Good-byes

I woke up from a dream and nudged Sweetness awake. She turned and put her arm around me. It was so hot, even the flies weren't moving. I heard a woman calling out on the street for somebody to come home.

"I dreamed I was riding in a balloon and had left the earth forever. I was waving to everybody I knew. I didn't want to go, but I thought it wouldn't be so bad."

"Was I there, waving?" Sweetness asked.

"No, you weren't there." That was the one thing that had bothered me about the dream. I didn't tell her that, though.

I said, "Maybe you were beside me."

Sweetness smiled, stood up, and kicked off the high-heeled shoes.

"Maybe," she said. "Maybe."

ALSO AVAILABLE IN DELL LAUREL-LEAF BOOKS:

ANGELA JOHNSON

gone from home

short takes

For
Crystal, Denesha, Jenny,
Marcia, and Wende—
Batgirls all

Published by
Dell Laurel-Leaf
an imprint of
Random House Children's Books
a division of Random House, Inc.
1540 Broadway
New York, New York 10036

Originally published in hardcover as a Richard Jackson Book by DK Ink, an imprint of DK Publishing, Inc., in 1998. Published in paperback by Alfred A. Knopf, a division of Random House, Inc., in 2000.

"Flying Home," in a somewhat different form, first appeared in *But That's Another Story,* edited by Sandy Asher (New York: Walker and Company, 1996). Lyrics on page 93 from "Talk to the Animals" by Leslie Bricusse. Copyright © 1994 Cherry Lane Music Co.

Visit us on the Web! www.randomhouse.com/teens

Educators and librarians, for a variety of teaching tools, visit us at www.randomhouse.com/teachers

ISBN: 0-440-22942-1

RL: 5.7

Reprinted by arrangement with DK Ink, an imprint of DK Publishing, Inc.

Printed in the United States of America

December 2001

10 9 8 7 6 5 4 3 2 1

OPM

contents

gone from home

sweetness

Sweetness found a baby once in the fur-
nace room of an old burned-out building
by the city bus garage. The baby was
wrapped in a blanket and had only a diaper
on. (Sweetness used to hang out there
'cause it was quiet, something her house
never was.) She picked the baby up and it
started to cry. Sweetness figured it was glad
to see someone; anyone.

She waited right there. That's what she
told me. She'd even left the baby for a
minute in the building and called her mom
on a nearby pay phone, to tell her she'd
found a baby. Her mom hung up on her.

She went back to the building, but the

afternoon got dark and nobody came. The baby stopped crying, smiled, and slept. Sweetness held the baby the whole night long.

In the morning she found a box near the building and put the baby in it. She said the baby was real wet by then, but kept smiling at her as she walked the ten blocks to the police station. Sweetness looked all around before she left the baby on the station steps. She called the station from across the street at a doughnut shop. And a few seconds later a cop came out and took the baby back in with him.

Sweetness told me a long time after that she wasn't ever going to have kids. She said she didn't know what made people do what they did. Nobody in the world should do something so sick as to leave a little baby alone. . . .

An hour after she dropped the baby off, Sweetness robbed a convenience store with a gun she'd stolen from one of her uncles. She'd never been in trouble before and it was a long time before I understood. She was calling out for help. Mama said she was, but nobody heard her; not even her mom.

The kid minding the store said he could barely see Sweetness from behind the high counter, but he could see the gun. She got one hundred dollars and a box of candy bars.

Sweetness said she never cried when they caught her, guns pointed, in the building where she found the baby. She had to swallow the candy bar in her mouth before she put her hands up and said real softly that she didn't have a gun. (She'd thrown it inside a mailbox after the robbery.) She said ten years old was too old to cry.

The cop who had taken the baby away held her hand as they walked her to the squad car.

That was the beginning. Sweetness stayed in and out of trouble. I'd get letters from her when she was in juvenile detention and foster homes. I waited for them; and I always waited for her to come back.

In Ohio you can bury yourself under the early morning cool dirt in August and not stay the least bit cool. Sweetness walks around all summer with one of those ice packs stuck to her head.

She comes over most days, early, and I find her swinging on the hammock on the screened-in side porch. She swings in time to some music my mama's put on in the house. Her sweaty brown legs aren't much longer than they were five years ago when she was taken away from that burned-out building.

Today she winks at me and pushes off against the wall and has fallen asleep before I can say anything much that would have mattered.

When Sweetness wakes up I'm scooping ants and putting them out a hole in the front screen of the porch.

"Reyetta. Do you think August is the most dangerous month of the whole year?"

I push the last ant out and go back over to the wicker chair beside her.

"I don't know about dangerous, girl, but it's the hottest. I guess it could be dangerous, too."

"I heard some old men sit over by Hannah's Market talking about how they can't wait for all the neighborhood kids to get back in school. They talk about how everybody is getting nastier and nastier to each other in the heat."

I put my feet up on the wall next to her.

"They should open up more hydrants."

"What? So the man from the city can try to close them and get beat up again? You know what happened—and he even lived in the neighborhood."

"Yeah, that was pretty sick."

I hear the front door slam and Mama calling to me.

She clicks down the front steps in her heels.

"Rey?"

I press my face to the screen so she can see me.

"Stay around the house today, okay?"

I start to get a big whine going before she puts her hands on her hips and points at me.

Okay was all she wanted to hear before she got in the car and pulled it onto the road.

I look up the avenue and I can already see the heat waves. Sweetness says it's like no day she ever remembers and it's just seven in the morning. She's already feeling restless.

I say, "You aren't going to get in trouble today, are you?"

Sweetness smiles.

Me and Sweetness set up the wading pool in the backyard and get out Mama's

Motown. We splash and dance around the yard till the water is warm. We dance for two straight hours, and lip-sync to Supremes songs, then get my cat, Moogie, wet. . . . Most of the morning is gone and we eat bologna sandwiches and pickles till we almost get sick.

Five years ago, when the welfare gave Sweetness back to her mom, the first thing she did was ride her bike over to my house. I remember how we pedaled as hard as we could to the Dairy Queen, feeling ten and celebrating that the only things Sweetness missed were me and ice cream.

We'd gone to preschool together and had pretty much never been apart except for the time she spent in foster homes.

We don't talk about what Sweetness does when she's not around me. I guess it's better that way.

I don't think I've ever seen her frown. Sweetness comes by her name honestly. She says "Thank you" and "Yes, ma'am" to my mama. She helps carry groceries to old people's cars and gives up her seat on the bus a lot.

Mama says the reason Sweetness is always in trouble is that her mom spends so much time in church, and not enough time with Sweetness. Mama says Miss Lorene can see God, up high, but can't even see her own child.

Sweetness once told me, "My mom is one of those high-heeled church ladies who sings gospel and hugs everybody with a 'Bless you, baby' and a 'Praise the Lord.' But she's the same woman who didn't miss me for three days 'cause she was at some revival."

Miss Lorene has found herself a quieter place. Away from her kids and the worries of the world. Sometimes she's in the house and sometimes she's not. That's about it for her.

Sweetness said when she was little she used to get on her knees beside her mom and pray with her. She said she used to pray to see God. Her mom would tell her that if she didn't see Him, she wasn't right with Him.

"So I went looking for Him," Sweetness said. "I looked for Him behind our house and in cars. I'd looked at Third Avenue Baptist first and hadn't found Him. By the time spring came around I'd been looking all winter and because I couldn't find Him—I refused to recite my Easter speech."

Miss Lorene had a screaming fit outside the church and Sweetness didn't look for God anymore. She just gave up looking, I guess.

My mama's room smelled like peppermint gum and lemons. Most of the clothes from her closet were spread all over the white cotton bedspread as me and Sweetness tried them on.

Sweetness had on one of Mama's strapless dresses and a pair of red high heels. She strutted back and forth past the standing mirror.

"I'm fine, girl!"

I grabbed one of Mama's hats and put it on her head. I had on a long, white silk blouse, dark round sunglasses, and no shoes. We looked at each other and fell on the floor laughing. We lay there and looked up at the turning ceiling fan. It was the first time that day I felt cool.

We watched the blades turn, then we watched each other. The last thing I heard was Sweetness's whispered breathing. I moved closer to her and soon didn't hear anything.

Once Sweetness told me I was all she had. She said she loved me and there would be no other person like me for her in the whole world.

Her mom told her it was wrong to love me like she did. Sweetness didn't understand it at first. She only got real upset when her mom said God wouldn't like her loving another girl.

Since Sweetness couldn't help loving me and was always wanting her mom to be there for her, her heart got ripped. Just ripped all to pieces.

My braids covered my eyes.

I woke up from a dream and nudged Sweetness awake. She turned and put her arm around me. It was so hot, even the flies weren't moving. I heard a woman calling out on the street for somebody to come home.

"I dreamed I was riding in a balloon and had left the earth forever. I was waving to everybody I knew. I didn't want to go, but I thought it wouldn't be so bad."

"Was I there, waving?" Sweetness asked.

"No, you weren't there."

"I thought you said you were waving to everybody you knew; and I wasn't there."

That was the one thing that had bothered me about the dream. I didn't tell her that, though.

I said, "Maybe you were beside me."

Sweetness smiled, stood up, and kicked off the high-heeled shoes.

"Maybe," she said. "Maybe."

We cleaned up Mama's room and Sweetness ran down the stairs to the living room. She picked at one of the old sandwiches we'd left and headed out the door. The sun was getting lower.

"Got to meet somebody," she said. Then she came over and took the round sunglasses from my pocket, hugged me, and left. I watched her jump over the fire hydrant on the tree lawn and wave to somebody in a passing car.

She disappeared into the heat of the city.

Mama didn't wake me later to tell me that Sweetness was dead. This time Sweetness was taller when she put the gun up to the clerk's face, and she didn't dump the gun in a mailbox, so I guess the cops did what they did. . . .

Mama says she sat in my bedroom door for a while and stared into space. She said she picked some book off my floor and watched me sleep.

Mama says she's never seen me sleep so hard. She thought I was having a dream.

I was.

I was dreaming Sweetness was floating away in the balloon, leaving me on the ground, and I was mad. She kept yelling at me with those round sunglasses on that she hadn't really given up, she was going to find God. . . .

barns

Walter Hamilton used to draw pictures of barns everywhere he went. You could tell where he had his lunch or got sent to detention. Barns. All over the walls.

Beautiful barns, too. He'd color them in and would talk to you about all the different kinds he'd seen, and where.

He'd talk about the CHEW MAIL POUCH barns and how he'd found out why the man who had first painted them had retired from barn painting. I listened because I was scared and interested.

We started figuring that when Walter wasn't in Juvenile Hall or in the hospital with some fight wound, he must live his life climbing around most every Ohio barn he found outside the city.

Most of us didn't leave the city enough, I guess.

Walter said it was happening in the country, though. We oughta see it.

We were all sitting on the lunch tables nodding our heads, and I was probably the only one thinking that there was nobody in the world like Walter.

This kid Marshall even whispered, "Who could be crazy for barns growing up off East Hundred-and-Third?"

Walter didn't hear him, and I was glad. Then he said something about one of his uncles having a pickup and he'd see us all in the park on Saturday morning.

Five in the morning looks like the moon, like nowhere I've ever been. Even the streets look clean. It's so quiet . . . like the first snow before everybody walks on it and the cars drive through. Pure and soft.

We are leaning together in the back of the truck—so we won't fall out from the tiredness. All of us brush blue flannel from the blankets off each other. I get to wondering how we could have been talked into this, but then remember that I wasn't. Nobody knew it, but I would have gone anywhere to be near Walter.

I watch him start up the truck with his dog beside him.

He turns and taps on the back window.

"Got room for one rider."

I see no one moving, so I start to jump out of the truck bed and head up front.

I hear one girl I know from study hall say before I leave, "Is this stupid?"

Everybody but me nods. I open the door to the cab and slide in beside Walter's dog. He smiles. Walter, not the dog. Then all I can think of is: Can farm animals bite, and how beautiful the city looks, left behind in the mist, and how I want to hold Walter's hand (forget that!).

Then we're beyond the middle of nowhere.

Walter passes out Styrofoam cups of sweet cream coffee that he empties from a big thermos. He smiles at all of us and it's like he's putting a blanket just out of the dryer over me.

A few minutes before, he'd driven the truck off the paved road onto this dirt one. I look over at Walter and daydream that we've driven alone into the country. We're having a picnic by the road. . . .

Walter is talking.

Now ten city kids from in and around East 103rd Street start listening to a lecture about barns. Barn usage and color. Barn statistics and the ages of barns in the state of Ohio. We are wide-eyed and slurp the hot coffee like it's the only thing keeping us alive.

It all seems like a dream.

Finally Walter is quiet and says nothing for about a minute. We hold our breaths and look at him—not the sweet-smelling wildflowers around us, or even the family of raccoons checking us out from across the road.

Just as I think we should clap or something he starts talking again. His dog even stops chasing butterflies and sits beside him.

I notice for the first time the scar across Walter's face. It runs from the corner of his left eye to his lip. I look at the tattoos on his hand and neck, too.

Two years ago Walter was screaming in the street, trying to make his little cousin breathe after she got shot in a driveby. They say he begged people to do something to help. He'd finally picked her up and waited for a city bus to take them to the hospital, even though everybody knew she was gone as she lay in the road. I was on the bus when he'd gotten on.

The bus driver sped up while everybody else—me included—sat dumbfounded. I shook when I walked down the aisle and touched his shoulder.

He cried harder when he looked up at me.

I was there when Walter started talking about how farmers used to help each other build barns. He talked about barn fires and crop failures and how even while the people were long gone, the barns still stood.

Walter talked about how most farmers were barely making it and how the barns were monuments to a time that would never be again.

Then he nodded to us to follow him through the trees we'd been surrounded by—and in a minute, there it was.

The barn stood tall and white. It looked so old. The paint was wearing off, and the metal hinges on the doors were rusty. A skinny tree grew out of its side.

Walter walked around the barn. He touched it. He said, "Think about them knocking down the old buildings in the neighborhood without a thought." Their time was gone, too. He turned his back on us and walked away.

I started crying. Like that. Out of nothing and for everything. It got so bad I was gulping.

Nobody moved or seemed embarrassed for me.

While I cried I thought about passion and death.

When we all walked back to the truck, Walter was sitting on the fender, smiling.

He looked at me and mouthed the word *Yes*.

The city isn't the moon anymore. It's another world altogether by the time we get back. There isn't enough room. I don't want to get out of the truck. None of us does. We sit together saying nothing in the park, looking at the wine bottles and a few crack vials.

An old skinny dog runs by, scared of us.

Walter's dog howls, looks at Walter, then wags his tail.

"He'd like it where we've been," I tell him.

Walter is the first to get out and lean against the truck, waiting for everybody to move.

Then I lean against the truck with him.

Somebody points downtown and says it was probably full of barns a hundred years ago. Somebody else says no—it used to belong to the Indians—then somebody else says natives and climbs out of the truck and heads for the subway.

A few minutes later the bed of the truck is empty, and I am still standing beside Walter. After a while I am leaning against him.

They tore down the building across the street from our apartment yesterday. Crackheads were hanging there and some girl got attacked in one of the doorways. One loud crash and it was gone.

I wonder if they tear down barns when they get dangerous, or just let them keep on working till they can't anymore. Cows don't attack people who get too close, though. Barns are safe and get to be old.

Walter was standing beside me watching the building go down across the street. He stood there until it fell, then walked away with his hands in his pockets and his head down. I ran after him. He grabbed my hands and I saw his soul.

I figure he was thinking about barns.

Just thinking about barns . . .

a summer's tale

See, it's a real hot summer day—so she walks, walks right past the Dairy Mart and the East Street Auto Parts store when it's too hot to walk. But it's too hot to stay in the house all day either, waiting for a break in the weather; and it's then that she sees him—not too short, not too tall. He's pushing a grocery cart full of empty egg cartons; she can tell they're empty because the hot wind blows some of them out of the cart onto the side of the road and she thinks, this man, he's got a story and, man, it must be a good one. See, she thinks that everyone's got a story because one day on the bus she found herself listening to a woman in a fur parka talking about what a bum her kid was, telling all the details, too, to a woman wearing a Perry Ellis coat—so she thinks, yeah, everybody's got a story and maybe this man will tell me his.

So she thinks, What can I do to get his attention? Then she backtracks to the Dairy Mart and gets a six-pack, runs up the street, catches the cart pusher, and says, sweating, "Tell me of your home life." And before the cart pusher knows what's hit him they're sitting under the Main Street Bridge, chugging on the six-pack and making sure the egg cartons don't take off in the wind.

"How come," she asks, flicking a spider off her and wiping away the sweat from her stomach, "how come you push that cart around?"

He says, "You know, you can't be too careful who you question these days, but I'm gonna answer you 'cause you seem real interested and you bought me this beer. It was a real hot day like this twenty years ago when I decided I had lost the will to live, and I went down by the railroad tracks to throw myself under the next train, but the train wrecked just a hundred yards away from me, spilling a ton of eggs all over the tracks and into the river on the side. It was the damnedest thing to see all those eggs cooking on the hot gravel and the faces of the engine men when they saw the damage, and I almost laughed myself to death right there. So I stole me some egg cartons to remind me how strange life is and how dumb, too—"

He shakes his head.

"Thanks," she says. "I knew it was a good one."

Later she walks up the embankment and it's still too hot to go home, so she goes back to the Dairy Mart for another six-pack and sits alone at the side of the road watching a road crew tear up a parking lot that's bubbling in the heat.

She salutes the GRADE A sign in the Dairy Mart window, the egg, the essence of life. . . .

home

After Ruby went away I used to feed Mingus, her cat, tuna tacos I got from Ray's Bar. You could go in Ray's and order food, but he'd stare you down from the door to the counter. He knew if you were underage. He always knew.

Ray has the best food on the river, and it's so cheap you can come out with a bagful. But Ray don't like kids. Well, I guess it might just be the kids who live on the river.

He says we steal and fight too much. He's always calling the cops and complaining to the city. Ray don't believe in homeless kids. Yelled at us all to go home one day when he saw Nik and Trey eating out of the Dumpster.

Ray started locking his Dumpster after that, but it's funny, he lets the cans sit out by the door a long time before he dumps them in. It's funny, too, how the food is wrapped real nice and don't look eaten off most days.

I got a job. I don't have to go diving too much anymore. I got a nice place to live since Ruby went away. I'm keeping it for her until she comes back, which I know she will. You can't just let places like this go up for grabs. You could never get the next squatter out.

Ruby knew that, too, that's why I'm here caretaking.

I met Ruby the first day I came to the river. She was sitting on top of the brick wall that blocks The Tides away from the rest of the city. She wore a flowered dress and army boots and was eating and sharing cookies with the seabirds that sailed along the wall. She watched me as I sat down below her.

I tried to ignore her—play it cool and all. She dropped a cookie on me. I picked it up and put it in my backpack and nodded up to her. She dropped another one down. We kept the game going till I had about a dozen cookies. Then she jumped down from the wall and walked away toward the old river warehouses.

The sun gleamed off the river. I unhooked my sleeping bag and put it under my head. I was finally here.

Ruby didn't know it then, but I started following her. I didn't have nothing else to do and it just came natural, I guess, following her around. Ruby didn't only hang around at The Tides. She'd go all over. That's how I learned to get around the city.

Ruby would get on a number nine bus and go uptown to the art museum. She'd always put a dollar in the donations box, then head toward the same room. Seems like she never got tired of looking at something in there. I'd never go in that room after her 'cause I was afraid she'd recognize me from the wall at the river.

I'd never gone to a museum before, but it was something to do. I started liking it. I felt good there. If one of the guards started looking at me funny I'd act like I was lost from my school group. This usually worked. That's how I got to know most of the museum. But I couldn't pull it off in the same part of the museum, day after day, what with the guards gettin' to know my face and all.

At least they looked at me. Most people didn't. In the beginning, when I first got to the river, the people coming out of restaurants and stores tried their best not to look or see. People in the city are so good at not seeing that I don't even think they know they're blind.

This old man who used to live under the bridge by Ruby's place was dead on the street for four hours, right in front of a diner by the Arcade, before anybody noticed he wasn't just sleeping.

When I decided eight months ago to come to The Tides I did something that probably saved my life. I got on the Greyhound bus with $489 strapped to my stomach, and I left Illinois as a boy.

I wasn't Pearl anymore. My family's got this thing for precious jewel names, and I was happy to be rid of it. I was Paul now, and glad for the first time that at thirteen I looked like the beanpole everybody always called me.

Not that it was so safe being a boy—it's just that people let you alone more. I spent some time watching the boys down on the river. It was another world. I never thought about acting like a boy. I had to, though.

I stayed at a distance pretty much until I had got some of the rules down. When I did, I was ready for almost anything. I didn't have any choice, I guess. The minute I walked down the sidewalk and out into the street away from my aunt Roni's house, the only choice I had was to try to find what I had lost a long time ago.

They got this furniture store on the river. I don't ever think I've seen such beautiful rooms in my life—like fairy tales, especially the bedrooms. My second week on the river I went there every day.

I'd touch the honey wood of dressers and sit on the nubby cushy chairs that sat beside them. I'd dream that I'd just got home from school and had run up to my beautiful room. Anytime, someone would bring me a pop and some chips and ask me how my day had been. I'd put my feet up and smile.

One day, when I was way into the daydream, somebody whispered to me:

"This beautiful room is empty."

I looked up in time to see a flowered dress and boots going through the honey wood living room across from me and out the front doors of the store. I chased the woman down to the river.

I was sorry to leave the store. It was warm and smelled good. Not like the basement in the apartment building around the block. I'd been staying there trying to stay dry while about three inches of dirty water fought me every night. I'd found an old trunk to sleep on to keep me out of the water, but in the middle of one night it caved in and everything I owned got soaked.

Now the woman in the flowered dress looked at me as she stood with her back facing the river. I looked down at my feet, 'shamed that she caught me chasing her. She stood a whole five minutes before she waved me to her. When I got a few steps from her she turned, headed past the wall, and walked toward the warehouses. I followed.

We walked up the back fire stairs of a white, peeling warehouse. It sat on a bend of the river. The farther we walked up, the more of the city I could see.

I followed about five steps behind. The woman never turned around. She acted like I wasn't even there. My footsteps could have been echoes of her own for all the attention she paid to me. When we got to the top of the stairs we were probably ten stories up. Ten stories over The Tides.

"Ruby."

"Huh?" I said.

"My name is Ruby. And yours is . . ."

"Paul—just Paul."

"Okay, just Paul. You're welcome to this place."

"Thanks . . . Ruby."

"But I got a rule. Break it and you're gone."

"Yeah?"

"The rule is to respect my stuff and me."

"That's two."

Ruby smiled and showed me her home, which she let me share with her until she went away.

I used to slide across the hardwood floors at Ruby's. I swear the place was about the size of a football field. One whole wall was mostly windows that looked out onto the river. Ruby said they used to store toys here. She even found a few boxes of them when she first moved in.

Trey says it wasn't like Ruby to just let a stranger stay in her squat. He says she knew who I was all the time. I say he is wrong. She couldn't have known.

I bet Trey his Swiss Army Knife, but it's a bet both of us know we can't win. Only Ruby can settle it. Even if she was here she probably wouldn't.

Ruby never did say much.

She didn't have to.

We used to sit on cold nights by the kerosene heater in the living room part of the place. Ruby would read and I would stare off into space.

Ruby knew the first day I moved in that I wasn't a Paul. I told her why I did it and she said she understood. (She always seemed to understand without saying too much.)

I'd go out and watch her as she sat on the wall keeping the river back.

Dear Crystal,

You didn't think I would do it but I have. I found her. It didn't seem like I ever would. I had stopped dreaming about it. I had stopped dreaming period in case she came up in my mind.

She's beautiful like you said she was.

You won't believe this, though. I'm

living with her. I couldn't believe it when she let me move in above the river with her. She's squatting at an old warehouse and it feels like you're in a boat when you look down into the water.

I think I look like her.

I see it in her eyes and I watch her all the time.

She disappears most days. I used to follow her to the art museum when I first got here. She loved the museum and would go all the time. I couldn't get too close to her at first. I was afraid she would catch me following her.

I love the museum though, now.

Sometimes I think about what it would have been like if she had stayed with us. . . . She could have lived on the street the rest of the family had stayed on. She could have dressed me up for all the parties you had to dress me for.

Her favorite food is cookies. You'd think people would grow out of that kind of stuff, huh? She keeps a whole bunch of them stocked up in a cabinet

she made. She says she doesn't want
to be caught on a cold night without
any.

I'm okay. I'm taking care of myself
and haven't gotten in any trouble.

I don't want you to be mad at me
again for going away and please don't
send the police after me.

Pearl

It was snowing when I mailed the letter to Crystal.

One ice-cold morning later on, Ruby woke me and moved me closer to the kerosene heater in the middle of the room.

Her face was a wider version of mine.

"You'd better try to warm yourself. If you don't, it's going to get harder as the day goes on." That was a mouthful for Ruby.

I moved closer to the heater and ate the toast she handed me. Grape jelly. Ruby said it was the only kind she'd ever eaten.

Me, too.

She was already dressed in a long black dress with red long johns under it. She had a nubby wool sweater pulled over the dress and gloves with the fingers cut out. She wore what she called her "favorite boots."

When I asked her why she called them that, she said it was obvious and laughed at me.

By then Ruby had taken me all over the city.

She'd shown me the cheapest places to eat and the warmest places to be if I was ever caught too far away from the warehouse.

Nobody bothered Ruby on the river. She was a queen there.

To get money Ruby would run errands for some of the people who worked in the offices off East Ninth. She said that was why it was so important to stay clean. They wouldn't have let her in the building if they thought she was one of the squatters living in the neighborhood.

She'd get tipped two dollars a person when she went to get lunches for the secretaries. She never got lunch for their bosses. Bad tippers. All that money, she said, and they were so cheap.

She'd pull me aside and tell me to keep my head up and look like I knew where I was going. I would look like I belonged then. Nobody would mess with me, she'd say. Then she'd grab my hand and skip us down the street.

* * *

By the time I'd warmed up and put my clothes on, Ruby was waiting for me at the door to go down. She straightened the hat on my head and zipped up my jacket.

We followed the river, then cut through a parking lot to go up out of The Tides and into the city. We caught the number nine bus and I smiled.

Me and Ruby in the art museum.

Ruby nodded to the guards she knew so well and led me to the room I'd never followed her to. We walked about six steps and sat down on one of the black benches.

Ruby took my hand and sat closer to me as she pointed to the painting of a woman sitting in a chair holding a baby. The baby slept in the crook of the woman's arm surrounded by gauzy material. The woman in the painting could not have loved the baby more.

Ruby held me closer and cried on my jacket. I held her till she stopped. We sat on the bench until it was time to go.

Ruby left me money in a can she'd set beside me the next morning. She hadn't come right out and said she was my mother, but she knew I knew, and that's all right with me. For now.

I didn't cry the way I'd cried when she'd left me as a baby. I'm older now and know people leave and come back—or just don't do anything at all. This time, though, I'll wait for her. Her note said—

Maybe not tomorrow or next week, Pearl, but I'll be back for you. I'll be coming back home—to you.

Ruby

bad luck

Once when I was walking down the street with my mom, I tripped and fell right in front of a man carrying a tray of flowers. Mom screamed as she watched the whole thing fall on my head.

I was covered in dirt and petunias.

Another man came by and started laughing because I guess I looked funny wearing dirt and petunias. Well, Mom didn't think it was funny, so she started yelling at him.

Meanwhile the flower guy wanted to know who's going to pay for the flowers (while looking at my mother), and the man in the deli wanted to know who's going to clean up the mess in the front of his store (while looking at the flower guy).

I figured this was the beginning of some bad luck for me, so I decided to leave the scene. Better to cut your losses and change your luck fast. I still believe that, too, even later, after a big tarp fell on my head when I walked under a ladder and got knocked out by a falling bucket.

I woke up in the hospital.

My mom was smiling down at me with a pot of petunias. (The flower guy had brought me to the hospital.)

Mom said, "Wasn't that nice of him?"

I covered my head with the white hospital sheet and growled.

Mom uncovered my face and smiled, then took a huge pastrami sandwich out of her purse to share with me, and said, "You're too young to be so cynical," just as the remote on the bed went nuts and threw my back out.

starr

I remembered her today because I went downtown and looked for new shoes. My friend May came with me to buy herself a black sweatshirt. It's all she wears. I don't think I've ever seen her in anything else.

We took the express bus downtown after school let out. May stuck her feet on the seat in front of her.

"Every time I get on this bus it's so full of people I can't get off at my stop."

She pulled the cord one stop short of where we were going, for the fun of it, hoping the bus would empty. The last person to get off at that stop wore her hair in a bun.

That's when the remembering started.

You can go all day and put all the things that hurt you away in your head. You never have to talk about them, think about them, or feel them. I've been doing it for so long and am so good at it. . . .

Sometimes when I'm at the arcade and I feel like I am totally gone from my body, it will happen. Or I could be at the park under a tree looking up at the sky and *bam!*

I start remembering again.

Starr used to take me to Venice Beach on the hot afternoons when it probably would have made more sense to stay at home under some shade, sucking up orange bubblegum ices and pineapple pizza.

I'd fought with Jimmy that fourteen was too old for a baby-sitter, but he'd just straightened his tie and shook his head. I like my dad, Jimmy, even though what he says usually goes; even if I hate it. He doesn't put his foot down much, except the time I wanted to paint my room black and buy snakes.

I guess since it's been just me and Jimmy, he's used to me and my moods and doesn't even look surprised anymore. But he wasn't backing down about a sitter.

Starr showed up on a mountain bike painted Day-Glo at our little house off Sunset. Jimmy took one look at her and closed the door in her face. He'd interviewed her on the phone, by fax and e-mail, but never in person. He couldn't believe the shaved-head and pierced-lip girl in the COOK THE RICH SLOWLY T-shirt was the Ph.D. in psychology he'd spent an entire lunch break interviewing.

In the end, he opened the door again.

Starr stepped in smiling and sat down cross-legged in front of Jimmy and listened to Basic Baby-sitter 411. She kept smiling, and in the end Jimmy and her were talking about seventies funk bands, and that gave me a headache, but it kept Starr in the house.

By the time Jimmy backed down the drive, Starr and I were eating peanut butter off of spoons and listening to some reggae she had recorded at some club off the Strip.

May says that I wouldn't be having as bad a time as I'm having if I had just accepted Starr as a sitter and not some kind of mother-friend. May thinks that you shouldn't get too close to anybody. She has three stepfathers, two stepmothers, five half brothers, three half sisters, fifteen stepbrothers and sisters, and enough grandparents that she opens gifts all Christmas morning. I figure she doesn't have to make friends. She has relatives.

May could be right. But after a few days being with Starr, it was too late.

I have some of Starr's bandannas. She used to wear them over her nose and mouth when she rode her bike. She said that the smog got to her. She had tons of them, all different colors and sizes. She never picked them to match what she was wearing. She picked them by how she felt when she got up and what she remembered about the day she bought them.

(Remembering. She got into it first.)

Once we were at an open café on the beach when Starr jumped over the wall and walked up to a man in a wool poncho reading tarot cards. I watched her as I drank my iced tea. She sat smacking on an avocado sandwich in a folding chair, nodding her head.

The man took her hand and started nodding back. He pointed out to the ocean, and, just then, Starr looked over at me and waved. I waved but felt so sad and didn't know why.

After that we'd run through the water in our clothes and got so soaked we stuck to the bus seats all the way home.

Last summer I saw Starr more than Jimmy. When I woke up in the morning, she was there. When I went to sleep at night, she was there.

Jimmy trusted her so much he just sort of started living in his office—which is what he would have done all the time if it hadn't been for me. I guess it was like May said; Starr became my mother-friend. She was what I needed, and I guess I was what she needed, too.

I knew it the day we went to visit her mama in the desert.

I got up early and Starr was standing in the kitchen fixing chocolate-chip pancakes. She'd started sleeping in the spare room and pretty much lived in our house by then. It worked for Jimmy—who was already gone for the day.

"You up already, Nic?"

I stubbed my toe on the old Formica table

I'd talked Jimmy into buying at a used-furniture store off Van Nuys.

"Sort of, I guess." I rubbed my toe as I started to eat the pancakes Starr had put in front of me. She sat down across from me, sipping coffee and staring.

She said, "Would you miss me if I went away? I don't mean right now . . ."

I thought about it for a while, not because I didn't know the answer. I was just thinking of a way to put it. I mean I'm not like that, touchy-feely and always being honest about stuff like that. Jimmy raised me, for God's sake.

I chewed my pancakes until they had dissolved.

"I don't have to miss you," I said. "You're here."

"Yeah, I know that, but people do go. They go on and sometimes they even go back. I just wanted to know if you'd have a hard time with the going."

"I really don't know 'cause I haven't had too many people go away from me, except my mom, and I don't even remember her. I guess that doesn't count. I don't know—"

Starr started laughing and drank more coffee.

"It's okay. It's no big deal. I just wondered about it."

Starr played with her lip ring and got up from the table. She winked at me and started washing up the dishes. Two hours later we were barreling toward the desert, and I'd forgotten what we'd talked about.

May told me I don't pay enough attention to things. She said I'm not the kind of person who always has toilet paper trailing behind me, but I don't notice if somebody else does.

I loved the desert and Starr's parents. They were old hippies who made ceramics and had posters of Malcolm X and Margaret Sanger on their walls, and hadn't touched meat in thirty years.

They loved Starr and never said one thing about the way she looked. She was thirty-two and a baby-sitter. I knew from the way my friends' parents talked about their kids, Starr would have had a bad time in their homes.

All Starr's parents did was hug her a lot, feed me too many organic vegetables, and talk about the sixties. They showed me pictures of Starr when they lived on a commune, and pictures of them at some concert. They both had big Afros and were hugging.

Starr looked at them and smiled.

I got that sad feeling and couldn't shake it. I remember thinking I was probably just missing Jimmy.

On the way back to LA I fell asleep lying across Starr. I fell asleep to her singing a song I remembered my grandmama singing to me. It was just a song, but it made me feel warm and safe. The bus drove into the sunset.

By the end of the summer I'd grown two inches and was just about sick of pineapples. Jimmy got a promotion, and May got her braces off and started hanging out with some guy who wanted to be a rapper. Every time you saw him, he had a Snapple in his hand. Starr told May this guy was as hyper as he was because of all the sugar.

May says I always take too long to finish a story, and maybe that's true. It's okay. I don't think people talk all that much to each other anymore. I know they talk *at* each other—all you have to do is watch those talk shows. Starr wouldn't let me watch them. She said that it was porno for the stupid and bored.

Anyway, summer was almost over and Jimmy was starting to be home more. I guess that's what he got out of the promotion. Starr had started to spend most of the day looking out the window at the road. Sometimes she'd count the number of Porsches that went by, other days it was Mercedes or Jeeps.

Some days she'd just look out the window and keep repeating every half hour or so that summer was gone. That would depress me and make me feel lonely. I didn't know why.

Jimmy says even though he knew, maybe he should have been on it a little more.

The last morning Starr pulled up to the door on her mountain bike, she was wearing hair. Simple hair. Not purple, spiked, or any style I'd have expected from Starr. She wore a wig pinned up in a bun. The lip ring was gone, and she was wearing what Jimmy calls adult clothes. She walked in the door and held me. Jimmy took one look at her and left.

It's funny when you see people with bald heads. Most of us think fashion. I guess at fourteen you shouldn't be thinking cancer and dying. Dying and cancer.

She'd told Jimmy on the phone the first time she'd talked to him that she was sick. She told him she needed to be needed.

Jimmy cries when he tells me he hadn't wanted to be needed so much by me.

Starr and me rode the bus to the beach and walked along the water until both our stomachs started growling. We sucked down bean and chicken burritos till we couldn't move. Then we watched the show go by.

I looked at Starr in her adult clothes and wig.

"What did the tarot reader tell you in June?"

Starr sipped her iced tea and grinned at a man on in-lines with a monkey on his head. She loved Venice Beach.

"He told me I'd recently had a life-altering experience."

Then she pulled off her wig at the table and threw it to a waiter.

Jimmy bought me this bike for my fifteenth birthday, and two days later I painted it Day-Glo orange. He doesn't really like orange bubble-gum ices, but he'll choke one down for me. He says I've really grown up in the last year and it looks like I won't be needing a baby-sitter this summer.

I helped Jimmy straighten his tie. Then I shook my head slowly, even though I knew he was right.

a handful

I got this long scar across my stomach. Had it most of my life. I got it when my stomach scraped the cement on the bridge abutment that I almost fell over. My grandma patched me up and I don't remember any of it, and Dad says that's probably a good thing because it was one of the worst days in his life, so he figures if I remember it . . .

In a way I do. Not the actual day or anything. It's just, for the longest time I'd start screaming if my parents drove across bridges. They had to find other ways to go places or make sure I was asleep when the trip started.

The only person who could calm me

down was the person who saved me from falling off the bridge in the first place—my brother, Kevin. He'd tell me my favorite story. I must have heard it a thousand times.

The flying boy would climb to the top of his house and take off. He'd fly to the store for ice cream and candy when nobody would walk him there. He'd fly away to the carnival even after everyone else had gone home and the midway was quiet and the Ferris wheel was still. The flying boy knew how to get it started again.

He'd fly to the top of the big wheel, catching a seat with his hands, and go around and around all night long. Then he'd fly back to his bedroom only as the sun was coming up. Nobody missed him in the night.

When we'd go over bridges, I'd become the flying boy. I couldn't fall off the edge 'cause I'd just naturally start flying.

I'd feel safer and stop crying, but would still hold on to Kevin's hand, listening. Mom's shoulders would ease down from her neck, and Dad would stop gripping the steering wheel so tight.

By the time I was eight, I'd stopped crying and only shook a little when we crossed a bridge. Kevin would lean over and whisper the flying boy story to me then, 'cause I was embarrassed about still needing it.

Once I asked Kevin where he heard the story of the flying boy. When he told me he made him up, I couldn't believe it.

By the time Kevin turned fifteen, you'd have thought that he'd have gotten tired of me and the story. He never got tired, though. His face wouldn't change, and as we got older his voice only got softer. When our parents thought it was time I gave the flying boy up, Kevin just ignored them.

But the summer he was sixteen, he stopped going on vacations with us. He'd stay home and work at whatever summer job he had at the moment. I had to brave all the bridges alone from then on.

One summer I had to tell myself the flying boy stories, quietly and calmly all the way from Ohio to Texas. And then I tried remembering way back.

The first time I'd heard any flying boy story was the day I'd wandered off from my grandma's house and ended up a mile away, hanging on to my brother's hand from an old deserted bridge. Something like that.

They said he hung on to me for about four minutes. My father spotted us, finally, and pulled me up.

Kevin said I was too scared to cry. He kept telling me I wouldn't fall, I'd just fly away to Grandma's front porch. He said that I must have believed him 'cause I started nodding my head and looking up into his eyes. My eyes had been on the water beneath me.

Kevin never told me more about that day. I guess he told everybody else, and as many times as I've heard people tell it, you'd think I'd start making pictures up in my head about what happened. Blood. Bandages. I haven't. I can't see it or remember anything except the flying boy.

Only the bridge and the newspaper article are left to me. In the picture they printed I'm sitting on Kevin's lap. I'm smiling big and Kevin is holding on to me tight so that I won't jump off his lap and try to get the photographer's camera. Mom told me this.

My brother never said much about the article. My parents talked about how proud they were of him and how he was always such a good boy. And no, they weren't surprised. He was a fine student and loved his little brother like anything.

They went on to say that everyone should watch their little ones all the time. You see, they could not have survived if something had happened to me.

The reporter wrote about how nice and shy Kevin was and how it was apparent that I was a handful. I escaped from Kevin's lap right after the picture was taken and bit the reporter. I don't remember that either.

I think my brother's whole life was decided the day I wandered away from Grandma's. It's Kevin the responsible one . . .

He treats me like a friend, and I don't know how he manages to do that 'cause I'm not the easiest person on the planet to get along with.

I'd been kicked out of nursery school with the suggestion that my parents might want to get me professional help. My parents were upset, but I figured that was it for me as far as school went.

I could stay home forever now.

After that I got kicked out of a few more preschools. Mom and Dad agreed I'd end up in prison before I was ten. But Kevin didn't.

He'd take me to each new school and tell

me what a good time I was going to have there. He always did that 'cause he was a good student like the article said, and Mom never minded excusing him from school to be with me.

I was special—a problem only my brother seemed to be able to handle. I was a special problem because everybody decided I'd been traumatized by something that I didn't even remember.

So it went on and on that I was messed up and nobody could do anything about it except my brother. There was safety in knowing he could take care of me.

I had become the flying boy. Able to leap any devastation I'd caused with a single bound. Able to get out and fly over anything that tried to stop me or tell my parents.

I was the flying boy for some years. My brother left home and went to college. My parents moved out of our old neighborhood, for reasons the neighbors thought were obvious to anyone who'd ever been annoyed by me.

But a couple years after my brother left for school, my career as the flying boy came to an end.

I was walking down the street, when all of

a sudden somebody yelled out, "Get my baby!"

To make a long story short, when I saved the toddler from oncoming traffic, my world changed in a minute.

Mom and Dad couldn't say I was a good student and person, but they did say how proud they were of me and how this would probably change my life. The article in the paper even said how redemption was possible. (They must have talked to the neighbors.)

A few weeks later when my brother came home, he walked into my room with a sad smile on his face. Mom had sent him the article and my improved report card. (I don't know! The good grades just started showing up.)

Kevin lay across my bed and said, "I'll miss the flying boy."

I looked over at the article with my picture in it holding Roy, the hyperactive baby I saved.

"I'll miss him, too," I said, "but I know there won't be any shortages in the club. I've already told Roy a flying boy story."

by the time you read this

To the Ones I Love,
The decision was made last month, and once it was made there was no going back. It happens . . . Sometimes it's written in stone and there's nothing you can do.

By the time you all read this I hope that you take what I've done in the spirit that it is meant.

I can't say what I'm about to begin will make you all happy, but what can I do? My whole life has come to this point. I can't go back. I wish that I could.

If you all love me, then understanding can't be too far behind. You have all been so wonderful to me through my entire life.

You've been there for me, like no one has ever been there for me.

My first memories of you all was my first dance recital.

Mom was a wreck, and remembering the time spent getting everything ready for the three minutes I was onstage still gives me a stomachache.

Mom yelled at the caterers—and most everyone in the house—at the party afterward. I couldn't find a quiet moment, and I was just five and shouldn't have had to go in search of one.

But you were there. Bright lights, but soothing. You knew what to say and what I wanted. Beautiful.

It didn't stop there, though. My whole life has been better because of you. What about that horrible maple syrup accident I got in when I was seven? (I've blocked out the actual events leading up to it.)

My dad called you that time. He was yelling—afraid of what Mom would say when she got home from the outlet mall, I guess. You told him what to do, and I wasn't harmed in the process. I was so happy when he dialed your number.

Of course, I must thank you for all that you've done for the others I love, too. I may be just fourteen, but my parents believe in raising gracious children. So I must thank you all for them.

My brother would not be the man he is today without you. Without you, he would never have had the courage to face a sorority girl with a sports car. He would not have married that sorority girl and had my nephew Dmitri (whom I adore), either.

Thank you for my family's future lineage.

And my sister . . .

Good goddess, you have single-handedly enabled her not to be housebound. It's a miracle sometimes. Just when we think she has it all together, she'll come downstairs and *bam!* Complete chaos. It's not to be believed. (Although I've seen it many times with my own bright eyes.)

Though at first my dad didn't believe in what you did for us all, a few years ago my mom helped him see the error of his old ways.

It was a happy time for us all!

Last but not least, my mom. There was a time in the not-too-distant past when Mom said she thought she might have to blow the whole house up because my dad laughed at a dress she bought. (I lied and told her I liked it, but it looked like a tablecloth on her.)

You saved all of our lives that day. Mom went screaming out of the house. Her eyes were bloodshot when she left and her voice was real high.

It was obvious three hours later that she had seen you. She was a changed woman, relaxed and smiling—full of the latest 411 on everybody in town. (But even you—miracle workers that you all are—couldn't make that dress look good on her.)

Now, sadly, I must end this letter. I hope you can read my words even though my tears may eventually run them off the unicorn stationery I am writing you on.

Some people come into your life and do nothing but make it better. They help you see what you may become. They foster growth and health in all things.

You are those kind of people. . . .

By the time you read this we will have all moved to Philadelphia, without telling you because we didn't have the heart to say our good-byes in person.

Good-bye.

With much love from me—Noel . . .

to Missy, Mark, Tesha, Mark, and Candy at Big Hair and Sharp Nail Design Trough

flying away

It's our last day in Hopeville. I could tell when Mama got up, looked out the window, and shook her head at the field in back.

Brother and Cookie keep eating their Cap'n Crunch and singing to the radio. I wait a few minutes before I start eating. Know the food won't go down anyway.

Mama watches the backyard with one hand on her hip and the other around a big old coffee mug we gave her last Mother's Day. It's shaped like a plane.

Mama loves airplanes.

She always talks about one day getting on a bus, going to the airport, and just flying away. "Wouldn't that be something, Victor?" she says to me. All of us on the plane like that—flying away.

Mama talks about how she'd ask the stewardess for a pillow and a ginger ale even. She talks about how close we'd all be to the stars up there—flying away.

Another song comes on the radio. Brother and Cookie know it. They wave their spoons in the air and snap their fingers. Brother rocks back and forth on his chair and laughs when Cookie starts to do the same.

I watch how they get up and move closer to the radio—trying to feel what they hear, feeling bad that they don't know we're leaving Hopeville.

Brother and Cookie wouldn't know yet. They're thinking about the bus ride to school and what they'll say to their friends when they get there. Cookie's thinking about how she just got settled this summer and met a few people at the carnival last month.

Brother's thinking about football and how he wants to start saving for a car. Two years isn't very far away. The car he wants is red, and his eyes shine when he talks about it.

I know what they're both thinking. I

always have. I can hear their thoughts in my mind, but that's the only place I can hear.

I don't miss hearing sound 'cause I don't remember ever hearing it. They said I did, though. Mama says I heard sound until I was about one—then it went away. She says that the few words I'd spoken went away, too. But that's okay.

I feel so bad for Brother and Cookie, so bad for them having to move, that I clear their bowls off the table before they can put them in the sink themselves. Cookie smiles the same as Brother does. They're twins and do so much alike. I've always wanted to be a twin. I've always wanted somebody to hear me before I tried to hear them.

Mama comes close. She turns from the window and looks at me the moment Brother and Cookie leave the kitchen.

She knows I know.

They got everything you'd ever need in the By the Creek Road truck stop. They got toothbrushes with elephant heads and beef jerky. They got thick pencils with troll faces on the ends of them and T-shirts that glow in the dark. Mama laughs at something the waitress says and bites into a fried bologna sandwich. She says you can only get good ones on the road.

Cookie moves closer to Brother in the corner of the booth and rolls her eyes at Mama. Brother stirs his Coke with a spoon around and around, never looking up. Mama leans over and picks up one of my fries. She eats it and smiles at me. I smile back at her, feeling sorry for Cookie and Brother. They still can't understand about the leaving. They don't want to understand.

By the time Brother and Cookie got out of school today all our clothes were packed in the van, and Mama had told the landlord and our schools that we weren't coming back. We never do.

On the way out of town she went to the store where she'd worked and walked out with a big smile on her face. Brother and Cookie didn't say anything. I closed my eyes. I didn't want to feel or hear what was in their minds and on their lips, 'cause they would never understand the leaving.

Once, Mama packed us up in the middle of the night and had us gone before morning. She'd been talking about planting a garden in the front yard at dinner. Things change just like that with Mama. Always have.

I know something, though. I know why we leave a lot. Mama told me about it one night when the air was so still I felt like I couldn't breathe. I could have drunk a tank of cool water. Mama brought me a Popsicle and turned on the porch light so I could see her hands in the dark of the night.

Mama's hands danced to me. She told me about the mountains and oceans she wanted us to see. She told me about places that only a few people had been. She wanted us to see them. She told me it wasn't the place that was so important as the trip getting there. Me, her, Cookie, and Brother were special. Nobody like us in the whole world, she said.

Special.

Cookie's over in the pasture, sitting next to a cow, reading. Brother sits next to her, staring up at the cow. Mama looks across the highway, smoking. She winks at me from underneath her sunglasses. She's out of reach. I can't put her cigarette out like I usually do when she rests it for a second in an ashtray. I wonder if smoke makes sounds.

I wonder if the big trucks that blow by us make sounds, too. I wave to Mama to ask her, but she doesn't see me or my hand signs. She just looks ahead of us on down the road.

I've been saving things in a big box from all the places we've lived. I got postcards that say HELLO FROM HOPEVILLE, OH the first day we moved there. The woman at the drugstore smiled at me and talked for a long time. She seemed so nice I bought two. Brother thought it was funny but never did tell me what she was saying. The drugstore smelled like bubble gum and newspaper. Most of them do.

I always keep my box close to me. Never know when you might want to remember. Mama doesn't like to remember. She never talks about where we've been. Cookie or Brother usually just turns the radio up and both of them look out the car windows. The music must be real loud 'cause I can always feel it. It shakes me.

Mama just smokes and drives on.

They all leave me to think about mountains and rivers and places only a few people have been.

I used to think that mountains made noises, but Brother told me they didn't, and I don't know why, but it made me sad. We'd gone through the Rockies once, and I think that was the first time I missed my hearing. I just knew those mountains should have been making some kind of beautiful sounds. I don't know which kinds, but the sounds should've made everybody smile. All we got was wide-eyed and open-mouthed.

When we were really high up in the mountains, Mama pulled over to the side of the road, got out of the car, and looked up for almost an hour. She pulled me out of the car and put my face close to hers. She mouthed the words "It's like flying." I looked up, too. It was. . . .

We've been days on the road when we pull up to George, Kansas. I know this is the place. Brother and Cookie know it, too. They sink way down in the backseat. Mama makes a U-turn into a gas station, gets out, and starts talking to the man who comes over to pump our gas. Brother and Cookie are heading down the street when I look in the backseat again. They've seen a Dairy Queen down the way, and Mama is sipping coffee out of a paper cup, laughing with the man.

Hello, George.

If you know where to look, you can get a house full of furniture for under a hundred dollars.

It takes some time, though. You just have to know where to look. Mama always knows. In George, Kansas, it's Suzy's Used. That's all. Used everything at Suzy's.

Suzy watches me as I sit on one of her chairs. It's velvet and blue. I smile at Suzy, then she turns to Mama and says something. Mama buys everything she needs for our house next door to the Dairy Queen.

Brother and Cookie saw the FOR RENT sign in the window when they were buying Buster Bars. My room overlooks the Dairy Queen parking lot. I smell chocolate a lot and like the way the sign lights up my room. Anyway . . . we find all that we need at Suzy's. Suzy signs to me to have a good time in my new house.

Cookie's not talking to Mama yet. Brother talks to her. Mama smiles all the time now. We're someplace else and she's happy.

I've been spending a lot of time on the roof. Mama brings me juice and sandwiches when she thinks about it. I'll bet you can see a hundred miles from every direction out of George.

Brother and Cookie started school yesterday. It's a county school. I guess there aren't enough people here to fill a central school in town. They didn't wave to me when they got on the bus. I watched from the roof of our house as they found a seat and scrunched up together.

Mama says I'll be going to school in a few days.

I've met my teacher. She smells like oranges, and her eyes twinkle. I like the way her hands look when she signs to me. They're nice hands. Mama even seems to like her.

Mama's been busy getting the house ready. After one day in a new home, Mama makes it look like we've lived there forever. She says she can't waste any time getting us settled. Home is important—even if we have more than three a year. We never have lived in an apartment. Mama doesn't believe in them. She always says, "You gotta have a yard."

The first thing we do in our new homes is have dinner in the front yard. Once we ate chili in Minnesota in the middle of January on our porch. Brother and Cookie coughed for two weeks. Mama fed them cough medicine and laughed about getting used to the cold.

Cookie says Mama is crazy, even if she does find us good homes.

I know Mama is in the house hammering a nail in the wall. She's hanging up the velvet picture of dogs playing pool. She loves that one. We've had about ten of them. Mama always tries to find the picture wherever we move, but then she leaves them behind. There's a lot of velvet dog paintings in the Midwest.

Cookie and Brother can't get used to George, and it's been two months. They still aren't talking to Mama much. The house is sad here now. Mama feels the sadness. It doesn't leave even when Cookie and Brother walk out the door.

They don't laugh at the table anymore.

Mama watches them, and she is quiet.

Mama is beside me now. She got up here by climbing out of Cookie's bedroom window, just like I did. She lies back and looks straight into the sky. I can hear everything she thinks. Everything.

Brother and Cookie don't want to find new mountains and rivers anymore. They're getting on a bus today.

I wish I could have stayed on the roof this morning, forever, but now I lean against

Mama in the cold while Cookie and Brother stand ahead of us and keep stepping off the curb in front of Suzy's Used, to be the first to see the Greyhound coming. It will take them away from us and George, Kansas.

Cookie and Brother hug and kiss me when the bus pulls up. They put their suitcases and duffel bags into the side and blow on their hands to warm them. They both turn to Mama. When she nods to them, they get on the bus to Aunt Marie's in California. I run behind the bus as long as I can. Mama walks away in the opposite direction.

When I get home Mama is drinking coffee up on the roof. I watch her looking all over George. She looks in the direction of the bus that just took Cookie and Brother away. She sees me and waves me up. There's a little time before my school bus gets here. Mama pulls me across the roof tiles to her and talks to me.

Mostly about nothing. Her hands are stiff from the cold—even with the hot coffee. Some of her signing I can't understand, so I close my eyes and lie on my back. Being up here is almost as good as flying. You can see everything, and the sky is clear. You can look right over George into forever, and maybe even see the next place you might have to leave for.

When I turn to Mama there are tears running down her face, but all I can think is that she should be happy. She's taught Cookie and Brother how to fly.

souls

You'd never notice it to look at him, but my boy Mick is probably the closest thing to being Dr. Dolittle that the world might ever see. It hasn't seen this yet. But when it does, they'll write books about it and do interviews on cable news.

He'll end up on morning talk radio and people will start wearing T-shirts with his face on them. He might even get a tennis shoe named after him. When I told him that, he said it was gonna have to be a high-top, 'cause weak ankles ran in his family.

"That's not the point, Mick."

"Then what's the point then? I mean, what good is it to get a shoe named after you if you can't wear it? I'd want to wear 'em around everybody and even get some free pairs for the old folks. . . ."

It's best not to get too literal with Mick.

It's best he stays with the animals, 'cause we always end up talking like this to each other. I get a headache usually and have to leave.

Me and Mick have been friends since preschool. We used to hide under the art table by the fish tanks and eat paste together. Mick knew how to hide big gobs of paste behind the puzzle shelf. Then he'd get put in time-out, 'cause the time-out chair was by the puzzle shelf.

When the teacher found out why we kept getting in trouble—Mick chewed with his mouth open—she started giving us only a teaspoon of paste each day to share on projects. We ate that, too. But our days as artists were numbered.

When I look back at the scrapbook my mom kept of my schoolwork then, most things were taped, not pasted. Upside-down clown faces and cotton-puff bunny tails shone with tape.

Even though Mick, like I said, was going

to be the next animal saint, it didn't start off like that.

"Greg, Greg, you in there?"

He was tapping on the outside of my bedroom window on the fire escape. I rolled over in bed and sunk deeper in the covers. It was pouring rain outside, but there was Mick in that big old yellow raincoat he must have got from a fisherman. There was Mick, smiling and knocking on my window like it was natural to be on the side of a building at six in the morning.

I got out of bed, skidding across some CDs on the floor and an old plate of pizza that had turned green. (I'd have to sneak that one past my mom.)

I opened the window and slid to the floor, finding a good spot to go back to sleep. Mick dripped on me. Then he opened his raincoat and pulled out something fuzzy from the big front pocket on his sweater.

He kissed the kitten on the top of its head, then tried to feed him some of the green pizza lying by the radiator. I stopped him.

"Uh-oh. Man, where'd you get that cat?"

Mick's eyes had glazed over as he tried to feed the kitten some jelly worms it wasn't going for.

"Found him."

"You found him."

Mick kept kissing the cat's head.

"Found him over by the hot dog place near the tracks. I was looking for arrowheads—"

"In the rain, man?"

Mick put the cat on my bed and it disappeared under the covers.

"What do you have against the rain? You act like you'll get whacked by it, like the wicked witch or something."

I crawled over to the bed and dug the black-and-white spotted kitten out from the sheets. It curled up when it saw me and fell asleep in two seconds.

I shook my head as I watched Mick get untangled from some pants he'd just tripped over.

"So what? You took this cat. I mean, it looks like it's been taken care of and everything."

Mick crossed his arms. "You think so, huh?"

"Wasn't it?"

Mick sat next to the kitten and put his ear to its chest. He lay across the bed listening to the kitten's heart for about five minutes. I had pretty much disappeared for Mick.

When he gets like that I just ignore him and do homework or get on the computer.

Mick stood up and took his raincoat off. He walked to the window and pressed his lips on the cold panes. He didn't stop until my window was full of them.

"I rescued him."

I sat up. "Where did you rescue him from?"

"Don't you like his spots, man? I knew this cat was special when I first saw him in the window—"

I sat up straighter. "What window? What window did you see this cat in, Mick, and then rescue him?"

Mick pulled up a chair and started reading one of my history books. He acted like the French and Indian War was the most important thing in the world to him at that moment.

"What window, Mick? A butcher's window? Was the special 'cat burgers'? I mean, then I'd understand. Were there alarms and cops involved? Will they be visiting with my parents in a few minutes? Will you be hiding under my dirty clothes in the closet with this cat?"

Mick smiled and said, "War is bad."

"War is bad, Mick? What about this cat?"

"I don't think I'd go to war. Why would anybody want to kill someone else? I mean, if they want something you've got and they're willing to kill you for it, shouldn't you just hand it over and get out of the way? I mean—land and stuff. Who ever made that stuff so important? Everybody should live in apartments and not own land. There should be a big nature park for every building. . . ."

Mick talked and talked till he knew he'd won. I gave up and invited him to breakfast, where he saved some eggs to feed the still sleeping kitten.

My mom and pop were so used to him they just asked the regular questions. How were his parents? How was school? Did he still have allergies?

Mick just smiled and nodded while he kept dropping food into a paper towel and frowning at me when it looked like I was going to clean my plate.

"You're full, aren't you?"

I stared at him and kept inhaling my toast and eggs. I was always more hungry on the weekend for some reason. It's like I couldn't eat anything on school mornings.

When Mick kept staring, I asked, "What?"

Then he took my plate and said something about helping with the dishes. My mom smiled at him and shot me a nasty look, like Mick was the son she'd never have.

A few days later at the mall pet store, more animals started disappearing out of the window and the cages. It was like somebody had a key or something, the store manager said. Everybody wondered who was taking the dogs and cats, gerbils and birds. Whoever was doing it, was doing it in plain sight. Mick told me that. After he'd found the black-and-white kitten, the pet shop was one of his favorite places to be.

He didn't hang out at the courts or arcade anymore, and he hardly ever stopped by the house. It wasn't like I could tell him I missed his big goofy face or anything. So I just did stuff with other people when I could.

I hadn't seen Mick outside of school for about three weeks when I got a telephone call in the middle of "Jeopardy!" on a Tuesday night. Mick was in an old deserted building by the tracks. It used to be Dan's Sweet Shack—one of the stores that the mall bankrupted.

By the time I'd gotten around to the back

of the building, Mick was surrounded by about ten dogs and a couple of puppies. Who knew what kinds they were? Mick was smiling and letting them out of these cages. It's a good thing there was a fence keeping them from the tracks, though.

The dogs were jumping around and smelling each other. Mick fed one of them something from his hand.

"Come on, man." Mick smiled. "Hang out with me."

I smirked back.

My pop says sometimes, if you trust the person who asks, you should do a favor for him—no questions asked. You shouldn't make it a habit, though. With Mick standing behind that old building by the tracks like that and all the dogs at his feet, what was I going to do?

Dan's Sweet Shack had become something else. The dogs followed us in, sort of. Mick flicked on a light.

Birds flew around the place. Mick frees them when he gets them here.

The puppies took off, yapping.

"I come three times a day and let the dogs out in the back, where it's fenced. It feels like a jungle, doesn't it? I put the plants in here myself."

Mick walked around patting dog heads and chirping at the birds. There was a knock at the back door, then a little kid peeked in from the darkness. He looked at me and then Mick.

"Hamster," he said.

Mick walked over to the counter, took a hamster out of a cardboard box, and handed the kid the wiggling furry thing. The little boy ran out smiling.

Mick had that goofy look on his face again.

"Pretty cool, huh?"

I sat down beside Mick on the floor. I shook my head and scratched a beagle on the belly. He wiggled on his back and closed his eyes. He fell asleep snoring.

"I free them—then give them away for free," Mick said. "To schools, little kids, whoever. I can't stand to see them behind glass and wire. I used to cry when I was real little and my dad would take me to the pet store or the zoo."

"Maybe he didn't understand."

"No, he understood. He wanted to get me over it, I guess."

"Didn't work, huh?"

Mick stood and picked the sleeping beagle up and carried him to a milk crate stuffed with an old blanket.

"No, it didn't."

I looked around and figured the cops were going to walk in and bust us any minute.

You got to be ready for a life of crime.

At Pet Pourri it took us about ten minutes to net all the goldfish who would have been lunch for the cannibals in the tank next door. We hadn't run into any security system yet. I don't know if it was just luck or if we were that fast.

Mick says the animals are watching over us.

I say the pet store owners don't live in the nineties.

My dad would have wondered what insurance company would give them a policy.

We climbed out the window with twelve bags of goldfish.

I started to feel like Robin Hood. I robbed from the cagers and gave to the animal-less. I told Mick this as he was crawling out the window of a pet store near the suburbs— handing me down a bulldog. It was going to a man down the street from him. His old bulldog had died last year. But Mick looked at it different.

He just said, "How could it ever be right to sell a being with a soul?"

Mick didn't seem scared at all.

Mick's grandfather had owned a hardware store. He'd made keys for people for forty years and had a ring with about a thousand different keys on it. He gave it to Mick when he was five. And there are only so many locks.

I swear, after a few weeks, taking animals out of cages and giving them to smiling people just didn't seem like something wrong. I try to go with what I feel. I did feel guilty sometimes, but I told myself I was helping Mick.

Maybe they would think what we were doing was noble. I fooled myself (a whole lot) that they might, until one woman in a plastic apron gave an interview in the paper on page five, and said it was probably some sickies sacrificing the poor pets for some cult or something.

That got Mick crying. He wrote the woman a letter and told her all the animals had good homes. He made the paper, too.

But we stopped rescuing souls for a couple of months.

"No wonder dogs bite. They probably have stiff necks, bending them to look in our faces all the time."

"Sounds good to me," I say.

"They're better off not being us, I guess," Mick says.

I watch some little kids screaming and going after some ducks who are unlucky enough to be out of the pond, and I think about them being better off than us. I look over at Mick looking at the world from a dog's-eye view.

He's going around with that look again, and I figure, right then and there, we probably will be crawling through some pet store windows soon.

It rained all day the last time me and Mick went out to a pet store. The rain gutters were spilling over, and the pitter-patter on the road had put me to sleep in algebra class. We were all walking around in a dream. I noticed that.

I left my room by the fire escape and stopped at Eddie's Big Burger to get myself some chili fries and wait for Mick. He came into Eddie's dressed in his long yellow raincoat—the pockets stuffed with something—and slurped down a cup of hot chocolate.

He had decided that we'd catch the bus to Chesterland and go to the Pet Hutch. Mick said he wanted to save all the feeder fish in the store, and that's what we were doing when we heard a key in the front door of the place.

We lay on our stomachs and didn't breathe. We were in the back of the store, and whoever was in the front found what he wanted there, rustled something for a couple of minutes, then left again, never turning a light on. The fish tanks already lit up the store.

The moon had come out.

Fish shined like shimmering gold leaves as we let them go down the creek, heading for the duck pond. Mick stood in water up to his knees and sang them a song. Something about "go away—far away"; I couldn't really follow it. He stuffed the plastic bags in his raincoat pocket and waved the fish goodbye.

We walked back home along the train tracks. Mick glimmered in his coat like one of the fish.

"Been thinking, Greg," he said.

"Yeah?"

"Do you think maybe we've saved enough animals—for now. . . ."

I jumped about two steps ahead, then turned to face him.

"Maybe."

Mick balanced himself on the rails, looking like some big, goofy bird.

"I been thinking . . ."

"Yeah, Mick?"

"You know I only started out trying to save the animals. Like I said."

"Yeah?"

"Maybe we ended up saving people's souls. Maybe for every animal I took so it couldn't be sold, we saved a little bit of the pet store owner's soul."

I looked at Mick and grinned.

Mick said, "I'll have to think about that."

He ran ahead of me and started twirling in the rain, singing at the top of his lungs—

"Walk with the animals, talk with the animals!"

While he was singing, I figured he'd do something, one day, somehow, maybe soon, to help everybody save their souls again.

With my boy Mick, you never know.

* * *

Now that our life of crime and saving souls and giving happiness to the animal-less is on hold—Mick is trying to find a true philosophy—I can say I miss it. But I figure sooner or later our parents are going to have to break us out of jail cages (or some morning talk radio show).

And they just won't understand.

batgirl

I used to be the Batgirl. Yeah, that's right. I'm sitting here telling you this, and you're thinking—this girl is crazy.

I don't mean the superheroine.

So now you're thinking—oh, she means baseball. No, she does not mean baseball. I never meant baseball. You have to explain that to people. When it got too hard to explain to people, I just stopped telling them.

What I really mean is, I stopped talking. Just like that. Nothing wrong with me or anything. No throat disease or whatever else they looked for. (My parents were for real about finding out what was wrong with me.)

And whatever they say, it was not in my

head either. It never was in my head. People think—teenager, Batgirl, *whacked*. Yeah, that's it. I know what everybody thinks. So I'm going to tell you all the truth, 'cause it's not like you live in my neighborhood or anything. It's not like you can point at me when I'm walking down the street or sit on the stoop and laugh at me.

I gotta worry about things like that.

So I won't even tell you what city I live in except to say it's on a big lake and they took the football team away a couple of years ago—which has something to do with the story, but not much. I mean, I can't understand why people went nuts—got upset, maybe, but they really went nuts. Anyway we can't go there.

Okay. It was a Saturday, and me and my friend Keisha had just got off the Rapid and were heading home from shopping at Tower City. Okay, okay. Tower City—upscale shopping, food courts, oops! Did that tell you the city? Forget I said anything about shopping!

Anyway, we got off the Rapid and it was near sundown, so we were both hurrying 'cause we both have paranoid parents who are pretty sure we will attract serial killers.

Before sundown in the summer, right after school in the winter. So . . .

This convertible came by totally painted with dog bones and real bad stuff on it about Baltimore, and the man driving with his top down was painted orange (which we were used to), but the really strange thing was he stopped the car where we were standing and asked us if we knew where the nearest post office was. While Keisha was telling him, I started swatting something away from my head. I'm thinking it's a big mosquito, but I look around and it's a bat.

Yes?! It bit me. No—not on the neck; this ain't no interview with one of the things. And I didn't all of a sudden start wearing great clothes and hating to get up in the morning. It bit me on the finger. It had just got confused, I guess, and was probably attracted to the music the orange man was playing. Something high-pitched and nasty. Anyhow—

To break in. My science teacher told me after the fact that bats don't go around biting people normally. They're pretty blind, et cetera, and she thinks I was right about it being drawn to the sound. There are a lot of brick buildings in my neighborhood—bats love brick buildings because sound echoes in brick.

(Also I saw a doctor after the whole mess was over. No rabies.)

So . . . Keisha with her Gap bag turned away from the orange man and saw the bat hanging off my finger and started screaming. She backed up against the orange man's car and fell into the backseat. She was still screaming when she kicked him in the head and knocked him out for a second. He hadn't put his car in park, so his foot hit the pedal, and Keisha and the orange man went flying down the street.

I started chasing after them, dropping all my packages, but not the bat, who had somehow gotten tangled up in my hair (probably when I put my hands on my head and started screaming like they do in cartoons).

Meanwhile, a lady across the street had seen what she imagined was a kidnapping and had called the cops. Keisha was still screaming, and I was still chasing the car down the street with the bat in my hair as the orange man woke up in time to plow into a city truck, then the cops, who just happened to be around the corner.

By the time all the cars stopped moving,

there was a cussing city worker, a hysterical girl clinging to a Gap bag, the orange man, two mad and confused cops, and a girl crying with a bat in her hair. . . .

That's the story. Yeah—that's it, 'cause I don't even want to tell you about explaining it to the cops, and how my parents were pretty sure it all had to do with me and Keisha being allowed out of the house without a guard (Keisha's dad said "keeper," really, but he's always saying stuff like that, so we just ignore him).

Anyway, me and Keisha will have licenses in a year and a half, so this won't happen anymore. And I won't have to worry about walking by people laughing at me, 'cause I can just get out of the car in front of my building and not have to walk past them.

Oh yeah, I started talking again. My parents looked a little disappointed for a second, but—whatever. You never know what might happen in a town that lets people painted orange drive around the streets.

a break

Leafy jumps out the back of Jamal's '73 El
Camino and runs up the drive, past the
potted hibiscus and the two hundred sunflowers growing in the front yard.

Today she hasn't seen Sophia. She just
couldn't do it.

When she was five, Leafy Rose Morrison
used to sell lemonade to construction workers. The Glen was being built then, and
Leafy Rose's house was one of the first in
the neighborhood. The spring before lemonade, she'd walk out her front door on school
days, past the green grass (Sophia Morrison,

her mother, was already into landscaping), and down the road to the bus stop.

Plaid skirt, white blouse with a school pin on it, and scuffed penny loafers—that was the way Leafy went to Willow Day School, where she used to wonder where the kids lived who went to night school.

But once summer came, Leafy stayed in The Glen and sold lemonade—lots of it. Her dog, Stickle, would pull the American Flyer wagon through the construction sites and along the dusty roads. Fifty cents for a big plastic cup full of lemonade, and sometimes even oatmeal cookies if she could get her mom away from digging in the yard.

Leafy's whole summer was selling lemonade and hanging out with Stickle.

By the next summer, The Glen looked as if it had been in the neighborhood for years, and there was an end to lemonade. . . .

Leafy still wears a uniform, except the skirt is blue now and she likes her nose ring much better than her school blouse.

She unlocks the back door. Stickle drags himself out of his soft bed by the pantry and sniffs at Leafy's feet as she rolls lemons across the kitchen counter, cutting and squeezing them for herself and using too much sugar in the end.

She turns on the TV next to the food processor, then slides to the floor to pet Stickle. Old dogs smell, and Stickle is no exception—which makes Leafy love him all the more. You should be loved most when you're old and skunky and can no longer chase the UPS truck and the diaper-service people.

The neighbors have never really liked Stickle and have had him arrested a few times. Mostly, Leafy knows, he's been persecuted for being free. The Glen has so many rules about what you can and cannot do that everybody at her house, Stickle included, more or less ignores them. The neighbors think Sophia is crazy 'cause she won't get the regulation mailbox or come to any of the community meetings. And who plants two hundred sunflowers in their front yard anyway?

Isn't there some kind of ordinance?

Leafy doesn't know why her mother even moved to The Glen. She paints portraits for a living, so to Leafy's mind they should be living in the Cleveland Flats or in the Heights in an old brownstone five minutes from the art museum. Sophia got left a lot of money by a cousin. Then she cut and ran from the city ten years ago to—as she puts it—a country cottage.

Hudson, Ohio, is not the country, and the house in The Glen with its five bedrooms and three bathrooms is not a cottage. Does she notice the expensive shops, boarding schools, and pizza delivery boys driving Volvos? Leafy doesn't think so. Her mother lives in a dream, and has never tried fitting in. Leafy has tried and failed, which still leaves her in the suburbs making lemonade after school in an unused house with an old dog.

And as much as she might want somebody to take care of her, all she's got is Stickle.

Jamal said he'd wait for her in the car. Leafy trudges up the ramp to the big double doors.

The place is like a spa, really. There's palms and the air smells like peppermint. And someplace there are wind chimes tinkling. But there's not one bit of wind outside, and Leafy knows it. She thinks: probably taped.

Her mother likes this New Age "rest home." She says the doctors are getting her back on her feet.

Leafy passes the "advisor" at her desk in the sky blue hallway. The color blue calms, they say; but it sure isn't helping Leafy as she carries a jelly jar of wildflowers to her mother's room. She knows what to expect.

First Sophia will quietly shake her head at the wildflowers in the jar. Why did she pick them? Next she'll ask if Leafy's taking care of the yard. Then she'll tell Leafy how she's recovered nineteen of her thirty lives ("found two more of them today, baby"). Lastly, her mother will remind her to call Grandma and let her know her trip is going well.

Leafy's mother doesn't want the grandmother to have the satisfaction of knowing she's had a breakdown—the word is, she's on vacation in France. A nanny (nonexistent) is taking care of Leafy. She's wonderful and is teaching Leafy Portuguese.

Leafy walks past her mother's room and hands the wildflowers to a woman in an orange caftan who's chanting by the solarium. The woman smiles at Leafy and anoints her with Evian.

* * *

The neighbors don't know that Leafy's mother is "resting." Her car sits in the driveway and Leafy moves it from place to place after dark. No one misses her.

Leafy does. When you get past France and the thirty former lives, Sophia Morrison is someone who grows on you. Leafy has been taking care of her for years, so the little rests her mother takes every now and then give Leafy a sad, lonely break.

And of course, when you have a lot of money, social services don't even come into it. A social worker in that neighborhood? She'd have to get past the Portuguese nanny.

Leafy walks slowly to Jamal's car. He doesn't look surprised to see her back in two minutes. He lowers his sunglasses.

"So?"

Leafy puts her feet on the dashboard, shakes her head, and says, "Not today."

Leafy figures Jamal's got a hard job being her best friend. She won't make him too miserable with the weird stuff. And anyway—he understands. What else is there?

Jamal saved her years ago from his neighbor's guard dog. He'd got the hose out and almost drowned the dog when it went after

Leafy. She started hanging around him. He hadn't told her to go away. That was enough for Leafy.

Jamal's family was big and happy. She wanted to be happy. So they became friends.

It's raining the morning Stickle can't get out of his dog bed. Jamal helps Leafy put him in the El Camino. Leafy sits in back with him. But by the time Jamal has pulled into the vet's parking lot, Stickle has stopped breathing. Leafy sits, inhaling the cappuccino coming from the coffee shop across the street.

The vet tells them: heart failure—which Jamal thinks is dumb; he says everybody who's ever died has had their heart fail on them.

He and Leafy bury Stickle by a creek in the woods and hope some developer won't be putting condos down there anytime soon.

Leafy goes to school and cries all day long. It comes to her that she didn't cry this much the first time her mother went away for a rest. Everybody understands, so much so that she gets to leave school early to go back to the house with the five bedrooms, no dog, and no mother.

Leafy sleeps in Sophia's car for two nights in a row.

On the third night she wakes to a bright light. She sits up in the backseat and is blinded by a flashlight her mother is holding against the windshield. Leafy doesn't know how long she's been sitting on the hood of the car.

Once, when Leafy was eight, she got stuck in a snowdrift in the front yard. The drift was nearly as tall as she was. She'd dropped down into it and thought, Yeah, this is it. Mom won't find me till it all melts. But her mother had noticed that she was a few minutes late—had looked out the window and seen a red hat thrashing in the snow.

She'd run outside in her slip and some hip boots and pulled Leafy out of the drift. After she'd wiped Leafy's nose and calmed her down, she'd sat in the doorway of the house rocking Leafy. Leafy wondered then if she felt the cold.

Leafy's mother turns off the flashlight and sits still and cross-legged on the car. Leafy crawls from the backseat to the front. Her mother is beautiful. She used to know that, but it's been harder to see as Leafy's gotten older.

Sophia presses her hand against the windshield, facing Leafy. Leafy thinks about her mother in a slip in the snow. . . .

Then she does the same.

Angela Johnson is the author of many picture books and highly acclaimed novels for young readers, including *Songs of Faith, Maniac Monkeys on Magnolia Street,* and two Coretta Scott King Award winners, *Heaven* and *Toning the Sweep.*

Angela Johnson lives in Kent, Ohio.